PLAYS FOR PERFORMANCE

*A series designed for
contemporary production and study
Edited by
Nicholas Rudall and Bernard Sahlins*

HEINRICH VON KLEIST

The Prince
of Homburg

In a New Translation by
Bernard Sahlins

Ivan R. Dee
CHICAGO

Library of Congress Cataloging-in-Publication Data:
Kleist, Heinrich von, 1777–1811.
  [Prinz Friedrich von Homburg. English]
  The Prince of Homburg / Heinrich von Kleist ; in a new translation by Bernard Sahlins.
      p. cm. — (Plays for performance)
  Translation of: Prinz Friedrich von Homburg.
  ISBN 0-929587-47-2 (cloth : acid-free paper)
  ISBN 0-929587-44-8 (pbk. : acid-free paper)
  I. Sahlins, Bernard. II. Title III. Series.
PT2378.P73   1990
832'.6—dc20   90-39776

INTRODUCTION

If translation is compromise, staging a play written nearly two centuries ago in another place and another language demands even further concessions. Still, the translator and the director must be aware of the danger of unwittingly applying our contemporary sensibilities to the work of another time—not out of some notion of artistic piety, but because we may be tampering with the very basis of the work's appeal. Failure to rigorously plumb the author's meaning not only exhibits contempt for his text but harms its presentation. On the other hand, the reason for staging the work is determined by the extent to which it still speaks to our own sensibilities. The director and the translator are left with the difficult job of transforming the work without violating it, changing emphasis to speak to our contemporary dilemmas, making cuts and sometimes rearrangements.

The theatre audience at the time *The Prince of Homburg* was written was narrower in class and more patient than our own. Plays ran longer and referred to a body of understanding that had to do not only with time and place but with implicit religious and political assumptions. What's more, like Shakespeare's history plays, *The Prince of Homburg* deals with real events. Most of the main characters were actual historical figures known to the audience. True, Kleist took liberties with dates, characters, and actual happenings, but the whole

3

struck a chord of reality for the playgoer. Since we no longer share that history nor deal with many of the play's assumptions, we look more to character and story in determining the work's present viability—and we cut. We cut lines that are now difficult, speeches that now seem prolix, scenes that for reasons of economy or story we feel we can do without.

While *The Prince of Homburg* is no exception to these considerations, it is so well structured that the scenes must remain. The only responsible cuts are of lines and occasionally of an entire speech.

Critics have been debating the meanings of the play since it first was published. Is the Prince guilty? Should he be praised or blamed? Is the Elector honorable or a villain? Who won the battle? Did the Prince save the day or allow the enemy to escape? Who is morally right, the Prince or the Elector? Who triumphs, the Prince or the Elector?

At the time it was first presented, the prevailing critical interpretations of the play held that it represented the triumph of law over disorder. A few saw it as a reconciliation of the law with a "higher" force, and in ensuing years this view dominated.

The editors share a third view: that Kleist saw the problem as an unresolvable ambiguity; that *The Prince of Homburg* poses a question without providing an answer. Such an interpretation explains the play's particular appeal to present-day sensibilities.

It is our reading that, in this wonderful play, we are dealing with a work that is unique in the pervasiveness of its irony, an outlook bred in the modern bone. While such may not always have been the author's intention, every major character

4

can be credited with a hidden agenda, a disparity between public statement and private motive.

Whether it is the Prince at the very last, peeking through the blindfold, exultant that his gamble has paid off; the calculating Princess, adroitly shifting her goals and tactics with each of the many changes of fortune; the crafty Elector, manipulating every ounce of the situation for his ends, or the ambiguous Hohenzollern, tacking with the wind, Kleist has created a cast of characters whose needs and the means they use to fulfill them—that is to say, whose humanness—are perhaps even more vivid to us than they were to his contemporaries.

Indeed, one of the major interpretive decisions for the director and the actor has to do with the levels of irony displayed by the characters. How aware is each character of his or her motivations? Which statements and actions are to be taken at face value, and which of them conceals other purposes?

Locations

Fehrbellin, some ninety kilometers northwest of Berlin, was a channel for crossing through the muddy plains around the river Rhyn. All the scenes take place here or on the nearby battlefield except for II, 8 and 9, which are set in Berlin.

Time

The action of the play takes place over seventy-two hours from midnight June 9 to midnight June 12, 1675.

5

Act 1. It is the night before the battle. The Prince of Homburg and his regiment had been ordered to leave at 10 p.m. Instead, Homburg sits in a dreamy trance in the garden. Here he is found by his friend, Hohenzollern, who calls the Elector. The Elector and his retinue play a joke on the Prince, then hastily retreat. Before they go he manages to snatch a glove from Princess Natalie. He awakes, wondering where the glove came from. The next scene is a briefing by the Field Marshal for all officers. Homburg, still bemused, pays little attention to his orders which forbid him to attack until signaled. He is further abstracted when he finds that the glove belongs to Natalie.

Act 2. On the battlefield, Homburg calls his men to attack though he has not been given the signal to do so. His victory is marred by a report of the Elector's death. This proves false, and Homburg is summoned to Berlin. He and Natalie exchange avowals of love. In Berlin the Elector places an astonished Prince under arrest for violating orders.

Act 3. In prison, Homburg's confidence changes to terror as he realizes that he is, indeed, sentenced to death, that the Elector has refused to pardon him, and that his grave is being dug. He abjectly pleads with the Electress to intervene on his behalf.

Act 4. Natalie intervenes with the Elector. Although he accedes to her request and prepares a pardon for the Prince which she herself is to bring to him, she remains uneasy. Her fears are justified when Homburg, given the option of freedom should he feel that his sentence was unjust, refuses to make that claim. Natalie sets in motion a recall of her regiment to Fehrbellin from its station nearby.

Act 5. The Elector answers the petition of his officers and the threat of Natalie's troops by summoning Homburg from prison. The Prince, claiming he is justly sentenced, demands they not intervene. Now, back in the garden, with a blindfolded Prince ready to die, the Elector grants an unconditional pardon and all prepare to do battle against the Swedish enemy.

Design Considerations

A realistic set is a matter of the director's choice. The only scenic elements necessitated by the text are the ramp in the garden and the hill on the battlefield. These can be accomplished by distinction in playing levels if a realistic set is not desired. Everything else can be achieved with lighting and, indeed, in view of some of the rapid changes of locale, contemporary practice would suggest keeping set pieces to a bare minimum. Projection could be fruitful.

In view of the specific textual references, placing the play in another period or country seems hardly worth the dislocations.

While the set can certainly remain simple, it does seem worthwhile to consider some authenticity of costume. The battle-ready field officers would be distinguished from the staff at the beginning, but would themselves be wearing dress uniforms at the church. The women's travel costumes should be distinguished from their court wear. The Byronic Prince would, in keeping with his character, wear clothes as a statement; as a prisoner he would outplain plainness, as a soldier he would be correct with a touch of the raffish.

7

Kleist, an early romanticist, was a major but controversial writer at the time of Goethe. Born into an aristocratic Prussian family, he went to war at fifteen. Six years later he resigned his commission and began a restless life of study, wandering, and, at age 25, writing. He was a master of the short story and wrote both tragedies and comedies for the theatre. He committed suicide in 1811.

The Prince of Homburg, Kleist's last play and his masterpiece, was first produced ten years after the author's death. It has remained in the repertory ever since.

CHARACTERS

FREDERICK WILLIAM, Elector of Brandenburg

ELECTOR'S WIFE

PRINCESS NATALIE of Oranien, his niece and chief of
a dragoon regiment

FIELD MARSHAL DORFLING

COLONEL KOTTWITZ, of the regiment of Princess
Natalie

HENNINGS

COUNT TRUCHSS

COUNT HOHENZOLLERN, of the Elector's staff

CAPTAIN GOLTZ

COUNT VON SPARREN

STRANZ

SIEGFRIED MORNER

COUNT REUSS

A SERGEANT

Officers. Corporals. Cavalrymen. Courtiers. Ladies-
in-Waiting. Liveried footmen. Servants. People
of all ages.

The Prince of Homburg

ACT 1

Scene 1

Scene: The city of Fehrbellin, 1675. A castle garden in the traditional French style. At the back, a balcony on the castle wall, from which a ramp descends into the garden. It is night.

The Prince of Homburg, bareheaded, shirt open, sits, half asleep, under an oak tree weaving a wreath. The door to the balcony opens. The Elector and his wife, accompanied by Princess Natalie, Count Hohenzollern, Cavalry Captain Goltz, and retainers, move silently from the castle and look down on the Prince.

HOHENZOLLERN: If I'm not mistaken, your highness, you ordered our brave cousin, the Prince of Homburg, to stay here in Fehrbellin—but only for the three hours necessary to resupply his troops.

ELECTOR: Yes?

HOHENZOLLERN: He must be tired from chasing the elusive Swedes for three days, so tired that the idea of facing General Wrangel again only adds to his exhaustion.

ELECTOR: Your point, Count Hohenzollern ...

HOHENZOLLERN: Sir, it's ten o'clock. The cavalry is mounted, the eager horses paw the ground before the city gates. But someone's missing. Who?

Who, but their heroic leader, our cousin Homburg. With torches, lights, lanterns, they seek him ... and where is he?

(takes a torch from a page)

There! Lying on a bench in a trance, fast asleep, dreaming of a glorious future when he will be crowned by the wreath he is weaving. Of course, you never wanted to believe anything but good about him.

ELECTOR: Don't be ridiculous.

HOHENZOLLERN: It's true, look!

(he directs the torchlight full on Homburg)

ELECTOR: Asleep! It's inconceivable.

HOHENZOLLERN: Fast asleep! Call his name and he'll roll right off the bench.

ELECTRESS: He must be ill.

NATALIE: Perhaps we should call a doctor.

ELECTRESS: He needs help, not ridicule.

(Hohenzollern hands back the torch)

HOHENZOLLERN: Ladies, you're too kind. He's no more ill than I am. I'm sure the Swedes will find that out tomorrow—on the battlefield. It's nothing but a temporary oddity of mind.

ELECTOR: Oddity ...? Come, let's take a look at this ... oddity.

(they descend the ramp)

COURTIER: *(to the pages)* Leave the torches.

HOHENZOLLERN: No, bring them. The ground itself could go up in flames and he would feel it no more than would that diamond on his finger.

(They surround the Prince. The pages light the scene with their torches. The Elector bends over Homburg.)

ELECTOR: What leaf is he weaving—willow?

HOHENZOLLERN: Willow, sir? It's laurel. As worn by heroes in the portraits he's seen in the Berlin armory.

ELECTOR: Where would he find laurel in this poor, sandy soil of Brandenburg?

HOHENZOLLERN: God knows.

COURTIER: Perhaps it's from the section where the gardener raises foreign plants.

ELECTOR: Strange. Still I think I know what's troubling the young fool.

HOHENZOLLERN: Ah, yes—tomorrow's battle. I'll bet he dreams astronomers are naming shining suns for him to celebrate his victories. *(Homburg looks at the wreath in front of him)*

COURTIER: He's finished it.

HOHENZOLLERN: Pity, there's no mirror. I'm sure he'd like to try it on—like a girl with a new flowered hat.

ELECTOR: I'd like to see how far gone he really is.

(The Elector takes the wreath from the Prince's hands. Homburg stares at him, red-faced. The Elector takes a chain from his neck, winds it around the wreath and hands it to Natalie, who holds it high in the air and steps backwards. Homburg follows her, his arms outstretched.)

PRINCE: Natalie! My beauty! My bride!

ELECTOR: *(turns to go)* Now let's go, quickly.

HOHENZOLLERN: What did the fool say?

15

(The courtier shrugs and shakes his head. They all hurriedly ascend the ramp.)

PRINCE: Friedrich! My sire! My father!

HOHENZOLLERN: I'll be damned!

ELECTOR: *(rapidly backing up)* Just open the door!

PRINCE: *(reaching for the wreath as Natalie retreats)* My darling, why do you run away?

(Natalie manages to elude him and runs up the ramp, but not before he manages to snatch a glove from her hand.)

HOHENZOLLERN: Good God! What did he take?

COURTIER: The wreath?

NATALIE: No, no!

HOHENZOLLERN: *(opening door)* In here, my liege. He'll look up and we'll all have vanished.

ELECTOR: Return to limbo, Prince of Homburg, to the void. Haply, we'll meet again—on the field of battle. You dream of winning that which can't be won by dreaming.

(they all file through the door, which slams shut as the Prince reaches it)

Scene 2

The Prince, puzzled and silent, stands at the door for a moment. Then slowly, with Natalie's glove pressed to his forehead, he descends the ramp. At the bottom he turns and looks back at the door.

Scene 3

Hohenzollern enters from below through a garden door. He stares at the Prince for a moment. A page comes through the door.

PAGE: Count ...

(Hohenzollern holds a finger to his lips. He doesn't take his eyes off the Prince.)

PAGE: A word, your excellency. *(pause)* My lord, please listen ...

HOHENZOLLERN: Shh! Not now. You'll wake him. Now stop babbling and ...

PAGE: Sir, his majesty, the Elector ...

HOHENZOLLERN: Oh! Yes, what is it?

PAGE: ... orders that when the Prince wakes up he's not to hear a word about the joke.

HOHENZOLLERN: Joke?

PAGE: The joke his majesty just condescended to play on the Prince.

HOHENZOLLERN: Of course, I knew that. Now move! Go on! Go take a nap in some wheat field.

(exit the page)

Scene 4

The Count of Hohenzollern and the Prince of Homburg. The Prince continues to stare at the castle door as Hohenzollern comes up behind him.

HOHENZOLLERN: Arthur!

(the stunned Prince falls to the ground)

Collapsed! A bullet couldn't have done better. *(approaches the Prince)* Can't wait to hear him explain why he's sleeping here. *(bends over the Prince)* Arthur! Hey! Are you mad? What are you doing here in the middle of the night?

PRINCE: *(still bemused)* Alas! *(recognizes Hohenzollern)* Oh, Heinrich, my friend ...

HOHENZOLLERN: Arthur! Don't you realize the cavalry, your cavalry, has been on the march for an hour while you're lying in this garden, asleep?

PRINCE: What cavalry is that?

HOHENZOLLERN: The Mamelukes! *(aside)* I can't believe it. He's forgotten he commands Brandenburg's Cavalry.

PRINCE: *(springing up)* Quick! My helmet and my armor!

HOHENZOLLERN: And where might they be?

PRINCE: To the right—no, to your right, on the stool.

HOHENZOLLERN: What stool?

18

PRINCE: I thought I ... the stool?

HOHENZOLLERN: *(staring at him)* I suggest you get them from the stool yourself.

PRINCE: *(noticing the glove in his hand)* Whose glove is this?

HOHENZOLLERN: I wouldn't know. *(aside)* Damn, he stripped it off her arm and she didn't even notice. *(abruptly)* Quick, you must go now! What are you waiting for?

PRINCE: *(throwing the glove away)* Right! *(calling)* Franz. Hey, Franz. That lazy dog was supposed to wake me up.

HOHENZOLLERN: *(staring)* He's gone mad.

PRINCE: Heinrich. Friend. I don't know where I am.

HOHENZOLLERN: In Fehrbellin, you lunatic dreamer, in the garden behind the castle.

PRINCE: *(aside)* Oh, God! Come night and swallow me. Sleepwalking again. *(fighting to pull himself together)* Excuse me. I remember now. The heat last night, you know, made sleep impossible. Utterly exhausted, I stole into this garden only to be greeted by Night herself with such sweet welcome as a Persian bride, her blond hair wafting soft perfume, receives her bridegroom. So I lay down in her lap.

(a single chime)

What time is it?

HOHENZOLLERN: Eleven-thirty.

PRINCE: You say the cavalry has left?

19

HOHENZOLLERN: Of course. At ten o'clock, just as you planned, the Princess of Orange's regiment in the lead. They've surely reached the Heights of Hackelburg by now. Tomorrow morning they'll act as decoys for the secret advance against Wrangel.

PRINCE: It really doesn't matter. Old Kottwitz is in charge and he knows every inch of the strategy. Besides, I'm due back here at 2 a.m. for final briefing. It's just as well I stayed behind in Fehrbellin. Let's go. Uh, the Elector doesn't know?...

HOHENZOLLERN: He's been asleep for hours.

(They turn to leave. The Prince stops, turns back, and retrieves the glove.)

PRINCE: What a strange and wonderful dream I had. As if the great doors of a shimmering palace, all gold and silver, suddenly opened and down a great marble ramp came the people near and dear to me: the Elector, his wife, and ... a third ... oh, what's her name?

HOHENZOLLERN: Who?

PRINCE: She ... the one I ... I'm talking about. God! Even a deaf mute could say her name.

HOHENZOLLERN: Lady Platen?

PRINCE: Hardly.

HOHENZOLLERN: Baroness Ramin?

PRINCE: Never.

HOHENZOLLERN: Lady Bork, or Winterfield?

PRINCE: Please! Can't you tell the difference between the pearl and its setting?

HOHENZOLLERN: Damn it, man! Figure it out for yourself. What did she look like?

PRINCE: Never mind. Forget it. The name has slipped my mind. It doesn't matter to the story.

HOHENZOLLERN: Good. Go on then.

PRINCE: If you'll stop interrupting me.... The Elector standing in front of me like Zeus with a laurel wreath in his hand, takes the great chain from his neck and winds it around the wreath. My very soul's aflame. Then he hands it to ... someone ... to crown me.... Oh, Heinrich....

HOHENZOLLERN: To ... whom?

PRINCE: Oh, no, not again!

HOHENZOLLERN: Who?

PRINCE: It must have been Lady Platen. Let's say so.

HOHENZOLLERN: She's now in Prussia.

PRINCE: Positively it was Lady Platen. Or Baroness Ramin.

HOHENZOLLERN: The redhead? Maybe it was the Lady Platen with her teasing, violet eyes. Everyone knows you like her.

PRINCE: I do like her.

HOHENZOLLERN: Then it must have been she? Still, she is in Prussia. Oh, well, you say at this point she held the wreath?

PRINCE: High over my head, like a goddess of victory, she raises the wreath with its swinging chain, to crown me as a hero. In an emotional storm I reach to grasp the crown even as I sink before her to my knees. But then, like mist from

flowered valleys scattered by a chilling wind, the
people round me move back up the ramp. I try
to follow but, as I climb, the ramp gets longer,
going on endlessly till I reach heaven's gates. I
reach out in vain to embrace one precious friend.
Suddenly the castle door opens, a great bolt of
light engulfs them all, and then the door roars
shut. I'm left only with a glove that I had
wrested from the lovely angel's arm. And now,
great God, as I awake, here is a glove!

HOHENZOLLERN: Really? Then this glove is hers?

PRINCE: Whose?

HOHENZOLLERN: Lady Platen's.

PRINCE: Yes, hers ... or Baroness Ramin's.

HOHENZOLLERN: And it was all a dream! Lecher, tell
me the truth. What flesh and blood romance
was played out here that left a glove behind?

PRINCE: No. No. *(looks at glove)* Oh, love ...

HOHENZOLLERN: Enough. It's your business. Call her
Platen, Ramin. The mail coach leaves for Prussia
on Sunday. That's the best way to find out if
your beauty's lost a glove. It's midnight, and
we've got more to do than waste our time in talk.

PRINCE: *(dreamily)* You're right. Let's go to bed.
(stops) One thing, Heinrich, the Electress and
her niece, the lovely Princess of Orange—are
they still here?

HOHENZOLLERN: But why ...? *(aside)* Can it be the
fool ...

PRINCE: ... I'm ordered to assign thirty men to
escort them from the battle area. I asked Ramin
to arrange it.

HOHENZOLLERN: If they're not gone, they're on their way. Ramin's been standing ready at the gate all night. Now let's go. It's twelve, and I need my rest before a battle.

Scene 5

Fehrbellin. A room in the castle. Gunfire is heard in the distance.

Enter the Electress and Natalie in travel clothes escorted by a courtier and ladies-in-waiting. They seat themselves on stage left. Enter the Elector, Field Marshal Dorfling, the Prince of Homburg (with the glove tucked in his coat), Hohenzollern, Count Truchss, Colonel Hennings, Captain Goltz, and other officers of high rank.

ELECTOR: What's that shooting, Marshal? Is it Goetz?

FIELD MARSHAL: Yes, your majesty. Yesterday Goetz led a scouting party to the front. He's already sent back a messenger to reassure your majesty. Even though a Swedish force of a thousand men has broken through to the Hackel mountains, Goetz advises your majesty to carry on and guarantees he'll hold the line.

ELECTOR: *(to the officers)* Gentlemen, Field Marshal Dorfling has the battle plan. Please write everything down.

(The officers gather around the Marshal, notebooks in hand, on stage right.)

ELECTOR: *(to courtier)* Has Ramin brought the coach up?

COURTIER: In a moment, sir. They're harnessing the horses now.

ELECTOR: *(sitting down behind his wife and Natalie)* Elizabeth, my dear, Ramin and thirty brave men will escort you and Natalie to my Chancellor's castle at Havelberg. No Swede will dare to show his face there.

ELECTRESS: Is the ferry back in service?

ELECTOR: Arrangements have been made. It will be dawn before you reach it. *(pause)* Natalie, my dear, why so quiet? What's the matter?

NATALIE: Uncle, I'm frightened.

ELECTOR: My child, you're as safe as you were in your mother's womb.

(pause)

ELECTRESS: When do you think we'll see each other again?

ELECTOR: When God grants my victory, as he will. Perhaps in a few days.

(Enter pages with breakfast for the ladies. Dorfling continues to dictate. All the officers are busily writing except for the Prince of Homburg who, pen and notebook in hand, stares fixedly at the ladies.)

FIELD MARSHAL: Gentlemen, the goal of his majesty's brilliant battle plan is to cut the Swedes' supply line from the rear, isolating their bridgehead on the Rhyn and leaving it ripe for destruction. Colonel Hennings ...

HENNINGS: Sir ... *(he writes)*

FIELD MARSHAL: ... has been ordered by his majesty to command the right flank. His mission is to secretly circle the Swedes' left flank, then viciously attack between them and the three bridges. Then, joining up with Count Truchss, ... Count Truchss ...

TRUCHSS: *(writing)* Sir ...

FIELD MARSHAL: ... joining up with Count Truchss ... *(pause)* who, facing Wrangel from the heights, has fortified an outpost with his artillery ...

TRUCHSS: *(writing)* ... has fortified an outpost with his artillery ...

FIELD MARSHAL: Do you have that? *(continues)* ... will aim to drive the Swedes into the swamp behind their right flank.

(a guard enters)

GUARD: Madam, your coach awaits.

(the ladies rise)

FIELD MARSHAL: The Prince of Homburg ...

ELECTOR: *(also rising)* And Ramin is ready?

GUARD: He is mounted and waiting, Sire.

(the Elector and Natalie and the Electress take their leave)

TRUCHSS: *(writing)* ... into the swamp behind their left flank.

FIELD MARSHAL: Now, the Prince of Homburg ... *(pause, but no reply)* the Prince of Homburg!

HOHENZOLLERN: *(whispering)* Arthur!

PRINCE: *(with a start)* Here!

HOHENZOLLERN: *(whispering)* Are you out of your mind?

25

PRINCE: What is my Marshal's command?

(blushing, he raises his pen and notebook and writes)

FIELD MARSHAL: ... whom his majesty again entrusts to command with honor, as he did at Rathenau, the entire Brandenburg Cavalry ... with the provision that Colonel Kottwitz is at all times present for advice and assistance. *(whispers to Goltz)* Is Kottwitz here?

GOLTZ: No, general. He sent me to take notes.

(the Prince is staring at the ladies again)

FIELD MARSHAL: ... will be stationed on the plain at Hackelburg, opposite the Swedish right flank and outside the range of cannon fire ... far outside.

GOLTZ: *(writing)* ... outside the range of cannon fire...

(The Electress winds a scarf around Natalie's neck. As Natalie starts to put on her gloves, she turns as if looking for something.)

ELECTOR: *(stepping towards her)* Something wrong, my daughter?

ELECTRESS: Are you looking for something?

NATALIE: My glove, auntie, I was sure ...

ELECTOR: *(to the ladies in waiting)* Would you gracious ladies kindly see to this?

ELECTRESS: It's in your hand, child.

NATALIE: Only one.

ELECTOR: Perhaps you left it in your room.

NATALIE: Dear Lady Bork, would you ...

ELECTOR: Quickly!

NATALIE: ... on the mantelpiece, perhaps.

(exit Lady Bork)

PRINCE: *(to himself)* God! Can it be? *(he produces the glove)*

FIELD MARSHAL: *(reading from a paper in his hand)* Outside the range of cannon fire ... far outside. *(he continues)* His highness, the Prince ...

PRINCE: She's looking for the glove! *(he looks back and forth from the glove to Natalie)*

FIELD MARSHAL: ... shall not, until his highness expressly commands ...

GOLTZ: *(writing)* ... shall not until his highness expressly commands ...

FIELD MARSHAL: ... no matter how the battle fares, move from his assigned position.

PRINCE: Now! I must find out if this is hers.

(He drops the glove together with his handkerchief, then picks up the handkerchief, leaving the glove in full view of the entire room.)

FIELD MARSHAL: *(annoyed)* What is his highness doing?

HOHENZOLLERN: *(whispering)* Arthur!

PRINCE: Here!

HOHENZOLLERN: You *have* gone mad.

PRINCE: What are my Marshal's orders?

(He takes up his pen and notebook again. The Field Marshal stares at him, questioningly. Pause.)

GOLTZ: *(reading from his notes)* ... no matter how the battle fares, leave his assigned position ...

27

FIELD MARSHAL: ... until the enemy, attacked by Hennings and Truchss ...

PRINCE: Who, my dear Goltz? What? I?

GOLTZ: Yes, you! Who else?

PRINCE: I'm not to move from my position?

GOLTZ: Exactly.

FIELD MARSHAL: Well? Do you have that?

PRINCE: *(aloud)* ... leave my assigned position ... *(he writes)*

FIELD MARSHAL: ... until the enemy, attacked by Hennings and Truchss, *(pause)* its left flank giving way and falling on its right, can only stagger backward to the marshes in whose ditches, we intend to see to it, those Swedes will find their watery graves.

ELECTOR: Pages, your lights. Ladies, my arm.

(they start to leave)

FIELD MARSHAL: At which time the Elector will sound the fanfare for the final attack.

ELECTRESS: *(as a few officers bow)* Goodbye, gentlemen. Don't let us interrupt.

(the Field Marshal also bows)

ELECTOR: *(stopping suddenly)* Look! The lady's glove. Over there.

COURTIER: Where?

ELECTOR: At the Prince of Homburg's feet.

PRINCE: *(gallantly)* At my ...? This is your glove?

(he picks it up and brings it to Natalie)

NATALIE: I thank you, noble prince.

PRINCE: *(confused)* This is your glove?

NATALIE: Yes, mine. I've been searching for it.

(she takes it and puts it on)

ELECTRESS: *(to Homburg as she leaves)* Farewell. Farewell. Good luck and God protect you. See to it that we may soon and happily meet again.

(The Elector and the ladies leave. The pages light the way. The ladies-in-waiting and the courtiers follow. The Prince stands still for a moment as if struck by lightning, then triumphantly returns to the circle of officers.)

PRINCE: ... the Elector will sound the fanfare for the final attack. *(he pretends to write)*

FIELD MARSHAL: *(consulting his paper)* ... the Elector will sound the fanfare for the final attack. However, to prevent an accidental, premature assault upon the enemy ...

GOLTZ: ... *(writing)* an accidental, premature assault upon the enemy ...

PRINCE: *(highly agitated, to Hohenzollern)* Heinrich!

HOHENZOLLERN: *(annoyed)* Now what is it?

PRINCE: Did you see that?

HOHENZOLLERN: Damn it! I saw nothing. Now be quiet.

FIELD MARSHAL: ... his highness will dispatch an officer of his personal staff to give the specific order for the Prince of Homburg to attack. Only then will the fanfare be sounded.... *(the Prince is miles away)* Do you have that?

GOLTZ: *(writing)* ... will the fanfare be sounded.

FIELD MARSHAL: *(his voice rising)* Your highness has noted that?

PRINCE: Excuse me, sir?

FIELD MARSHAL: Have you noted that?

PRINCE: About the fanfare?

HOHENZOLLERN: *(angrily whispering)* It's not about the damned fanfare! It's the messenger...! "Only then will the fanfare ..."

GOLTZ: *(parroting)* Only then will the fanfare ...

PRINCE: *(interrupting)* Yes, of course. *(he writes)* Only then will the fanfare ... *(pause)*

FIELD MARSHAL: Baron Goltz. This is important. Tell Colonel Kottwitz I wish to speak with him if possible before the battle.

GOLTZ: *(gets the meaning)* I'll arrange it. You can be sure.

(pause)

ELECTOR: *(returning)* Generals, officers, dawn is breaking. You have your notes?

FIELD MARSHAL: Finished, your majesty. Every detail of your battle plan is written down by every officer.

ELECTOR: *(taking his hat and gloves)* My Prince of Homburg. I urge you to stay calm. Recently, as you well know, you've thrown away two victories in my Rhine campaigns. Control yourself. I can't afford to lose a third. Today my throne and my country are at risk. *(to the officers)* Follow me! *(calls)* Franz!

GROOM: *(entering)* Here, sir.

ELECTOR: My white horse. Hurry. I want to reach the field before the sun is high.

(Exit the general. The rest follow, except for the Prince.)

Scene 6

PRINCE: Now, Dame Fortune, whose veil the wind has briefly lifted for me like a sail, roll on. Today, fleetingly, you smiled on me, teased me with the promise of spilling future joy from your horn of plenty. Now on the battlefield, capricious daughter of the Gods, though you be tied to Swedish chariots with seven chains of iron, I'll capture you for good, o'erturn your cornucopia, and strew its blessings at my feet.

(exit)

ACT 2

Scene *1*

*The battlefield near Fehrbellin. The sound of horses
offstage. They carry Kottwitz, Hohenzollern, Goltz, and
other officers.*

KOTTWITZ *(offstage)*: Cavalry, halt! Dismount!

*(Hohenzollern and Goltz enter shaking their heads,
muttering, "Halt! Halt!")*

KOTTWITZ *(offstage)*: And which of my friends will
help me off my horse?

(Hohenzollern and Goltz exit)

HOHENZOLLERN AND GOLTZ: Coming. Hold on.
We're right here.

KOTTWITZ: Curse these old bones. *(grunts)* I thank
you, sirs. I wish you each a noble son to help in
your old age as you have in mine.

(all enter)

Ah yes. On horseback I still feel young, vigorous.
When I dismount I fall apart, body and soul.
(looking around) And where is the Prince, our
distinguished commander?

HOHENZOLLERN: He'll be here soon.

KOTTWITZ: Where is he?

33

HOHENZOLLERN: He rode into the village—hidden back there behind the bush. He'll be right back.

KOTTWITZ: I hear he fell off his horse last night.

HOHENZOLLERN: So I'm told.

KOTTWITZ: Just like that?

HOHENZOLLERN: Nothing serious. His horse shied at the mill crossing. The Prince just slid off. Wasn't hurt at all. Totally unimportant.

KOTTWITZ: *(climbing a small hill)* What a heavenly day. Created by the Lord of life for pursuits pleasanter than war. One's spirit joins the scented air, joyous, soaring like a lark into the calm skies under clouds made crimson by the fiery sun.

HOHENZOLLERN: Have you found Marshal Dorfling yet?

KOTTWITZ: *(stepping down)* No, damn it! What does his excellency think I am—a bird, an arrow, an idea, that can soar over the battlefield? I checked the outpost on the heights, then I rode back to the rear in the valley. The Marshal was the only person I couldn't find. So I rejoined my regiment.

HOHENZOLLERN: He'll be very annoyed. Apparently he had something important to tell you.

OFFICER: Well, well. Here comes our illustrious leader now.

(Enter the Prince of Homburg. His left hand is wrapped in a black bandage.)

KOTTWITZ: Greetings, my young and noble Prince. As you no doubt noticed, while you were in the village I stationed horsemen on the valley road. I hope you approve my decision.

PRINCE: Good morning, Kottwitz.... Friends, good morning. You know I agree with everything you do.

HOHENZOLLERN: What were you doing in the village, Arthur? You look so solemn.

PRINCE: I ... was in the chapel. I saw it when we passed, half hidden by the tranquil village trees. The bells, ringing for morning prayers, called me to the altar.

KOTTWITZ: A pious young Prince, I must say. Believe me, the mission that ends with prayer will finish blessed and victorious.

PRINCE: *(drawing Hohenzollern aside)* I've been wanting to ask you something, Heinrich.... Last night, the briefing. What did Dorfling say about my orders for today?

HOHENZOLLERN: You were distracted. I noticed that.

PRINCE: Distracted ... confused. I get that way when I have to take dictation.

HOHENZOLLERN: Luckily, there wasn't much for you to write. Truchss and Hennings will attack the Swedes with infantry. You are to keep the cavalry ready here in the valley until you are ordered to attack.

(the Prince thinks this over for a moment)

PRINCE: That's a strange strategy.

HOHENZOLLERN: What is, my friend?

(he stares at the Prince; noise of artillery)

KOTTWITZ: *(from the hill)* Hurray. It's Hennings. The battle has begun.

(the others climb the hill)

PRINCE: Who is it? What's going on?

HOHENZOLLERN: Colonel Hennings, Arthur, is attacking Wrangel from the rear. Come on, you can see it all from here.

GOLTZ: Those are our troops along the river. Tremendous.

PRINCE: *(shading his eyes with his hand)* Hennings on the right?

FIRST OFFICER: Yes, your excellency.

PRINCE: Damn it! What's going on!? Yesterday his position was on the left.

(burst of artillery)

KOTTWITZ: Oh, no! Wrangel's got Hennings' men at point-blank range with a dozen cannons.

FIRST OFFICER: I must say, those Swedes are well entrenched.

SECOND OFFICER: By God, look! Their ramparts are as high as the spire on the village church.

GOLTZ: There's Truchss!

PRINCE: Truchss?

KOTTWITZ: Of course! He's coming to help Hennings from the front.

PRINCE: How did Truchss end up in the center today?

(heavy gunfire)

GOLTZ: By heaven, look! The village has caught fire.

FIRST OFFICER: Yes, it's burning.

36

SECOND OFFICER: The flames are running up the steeple.

GOLTZ: Look at the Swedish dispatch men—right, left, they don't know where they are.

SECOND OFFICER: They're pulling back.

KOTTWITZ: Where?

FIRST OFFICER: On their right flank.

THIRD OFFICER: Whole columns are moving. Three regiments. Looks like they're going to reinforce their left.

SECOND OFFICER: You're right. And they're moving up cavalry on the right to cover the maneuver.

HOHENZOLLERN: *(laughing)* They'll clear the field in a mighty hurry when they find us hidden in this valley.

(musket fire)

KOTTWITZ: Look at that, my men!

SECOND OFFICER: And listen!

FIRST OFFICER: Musket fire.

THIRD OFFICER: Our men are fighting at the trenches.

GOLTZ: God, I've never heard artillery so loud—like thunder.

HOHENZOLLERN: Shoot! Shoot! Blast earth's womb open to make a grave for all the Swedish dead.

(pause; cheers of victory are heard in the distance)

FIRST OFFICER: Thanks to the God of Battle for granting us this victory. Wrangel retreats!

HOHENZOLLERN: Impossible!

GOLTZ: By heaven, it's true. Look at the left flank. He's clearing his guns from the trenches.

ALL: Victory. Hurrah. The day is ours.

PRINCE: *(climbing down the hill)* Up Kottwitz, follow me!

KOTTWITZ: *(to the officers)* Be calm, children. Easy.

PRINCE: Sound the fanfare! Follow me!

KOTTWITZ: I said, go easy!

PRINCE: *(wildly)* No, by all creation.

KOTTWITZ: Our orders were clear at the briefing. We're not to move till we're commanded. Goltz, read the gentleman the Elector's orders.

PRINCE: Till we're commanded! Oh, Kottwitz, is your horseman blood so slow it denies the orders of your heart?

KOTTWITZ: Orders ...?

HOHENZOLLERN: Please ...

KOTTWITZ: ... of my heart?

HOHENZOLLERN: ... listen to him, Arthur.

GOLTZ: Wait a minute, Colonel!

KOTTWITZ: *(insulted)* So, young master, that's the way you see me, is it? Dare me and I'll drag your horse by my horse's tail. So! To battle, gentlemen. Sound the fanfare. Kottwitz is on the march!

GOLTZ: No, absolutely not, Colonel, not on my life!

SECOND OFFICER: Hennings' troops haven't reached the river yet.

FIRST OFFICER: Take his sword.

PRINCE: My sword?! *(shoves him back)* Insolent cub, too green to know the army's ten commandments. Here's your own together with its sheath.

(he rips the sword away, sword belt and all)

FIRST OFFICER: *(reeling)* My Prince! This act! By God, I ...

PRINCE: *(moving toward him, menacingly)* Silence!

HOHENZOLLERN: *(to officer)* Are you insane? Be quiet!

PRINCE: *(handing over the saber)* Orderlies! Confine him to barracks. *(to the rest)* Now, men, here are your orders. Scoundrels and cowards refuse to follow their general into battle. Which of you is staying?

KOTTWITZ: Why so upset? You know where I stand.

HOHENZOLLERN: *(conciliatory)* They were only giving you advice.

KOTTWITZ: Count me in. But it's on your head.

PRINCE: I accept that. Brothers, follow me!

Scene 2

A room in the village. A peasant and his wife are working at a table. Enter a courtier in boots and spurs.

COURTIER: Greetings, good friends. Do you have room in your house for a few guests?

PEASANT: Of course, with pleasure.

WIFE: May we ask, whom?

39

COURTIER: No less than our country's first lady. Her coach's axle broke at the village gate and, learning of our glorious victory, we need not take the journey.

PEASANT AND WIFE: *(standing up)* The battle is over? Glory be to God!

COURTIER: You didn't know? The Swedish army has been driven back. Brandenburg is rescued from fire and sword, at least for now, if not forever. But look, here comes her majesty.

Scene 3

Enter the Electress, pale and agitated. Princess Natalie and several ladies follow.

ELECTRESS: *(at the threshold)* Bork! Winterfeld! Give me your arm.

NATALIE: *(hurrying to her)* Oh, my dear mother.

LADIES-IN-WAITING: *(supporting her)* She's fainting. Look how pale she is.

ELECTRESS: A chair! I must sit down. Dead? Did he say, dead?

NATALIE: My dear mother ...

ELECTRESS: I'll hear it from the messenger of death himself.

Scene 4

Enter Captain Morner, wounded, supported by two cavalrymen.

ELECTRESS: What news do you bring, dreaded messenger?

MORNER: Sadly, dear lady, what I witnessed with my own eyes to my eternal grief.

ELECTRESS: I'll hear it all. Proceed.

MORNER: The Elector is taken from us.

NATALIE: Oh, heaven! Must we endure this terrible blow? *(she buries her face in her hands)*

ELECTRESS: They say that just before the lightning strikes a wanderer, the murderous bolt lights up his world in one last purple glow. So be your words. Tell me exactly how he died, then come night to finish me forever.

(guided by the two cavalrymen, Morner moves closer)

MORNER: As soon as the Swedes, under heavy attack by Truchss, had started their retreat, the Prince of Homburg made a frontal assault against Wrangel on the plain. His cavalry had broken through two enemy lines, destroying every fleeing Swede. But then he found himself looking down the deadly barrels of an artillery battalion, pounded by a murderous barrage of shells. His men were flattened like a wheat field in a storm.

41

Finally, between some hills and trees he stopped
to marshal his scattered soldiers.

NATALIE: My dearest, steel yourself.

ELECTRESS: Let me be.

MORNER: Then, just as we are struggling from the
dust, we see his majesty advancing on the enemy, surrounded by the battle flags of Truchss's
company. Radiant, astride his great white horse,
he lights the path to victory like the sun.
Regrouped on a hilltop, we marvel at the sight
when suddenly, a great bombardment. The horse
and rider fall before our very eyes. Two stan-
dard bearers, falling over him, then hide our
majesty from view.

NATALIE: Enough, my darling.

LADY-IN-WAITING: Merciful heaven.

ELECTRESS: Go on. Go on.

MORNER: The Prince, in dreadful agony at this
sight, charges towards the Swedish trenches, bursting with fury like a baited bear, vowing revenge,
and we with him, flying across walls and ditches.
The enemy is slain or scattered, his cannon,
flags, drums, and standards, all his battle gear
in fact is captured. And had there been no
bridgehead on the Rhyn, no Swede would be
left alive to tell his children how the great Elector of Brandenburg fell at Fehrbellin.

ELECTRESS: It cost too much to buy this victory. Give
me back the price you paid. *(she faints)*

LADY-IN-WAITING: Oh God! She's fainted.

(Natalie weeps)

42

Scene 5

The Prince of Homburg enters.

PRINCE: Natalie, my precious. *(deeply moved, he lays her hand on his heart)*

NATALIE: So it's true?

PRINCE: If only I could say no. If I could only with the blood of my own heart bring him back to life again.

NATALIE: *(drying her tears)* Have they found the body yet?

PRINCE: Until this moment, lust for vengeance fixed me on destroying Wrangel. But I have sent a detachment to seek his highness's body on the field of death. I'm certain it will be here by nightfall.

NATALIE: Now who is left to stem the Swedes in this abhorrent war? His fame and fortune made us many enemies. Who will defend us now?

PRINCE: *(taking her hand)* I will. I. Dear lady, for your sweet sake, that mission shall be mine. Like an angel with flaming sword, I will protect this throne, made so untimely empty. His wish was a free Brandenburg by year's end. I swear to make that wish come true.

NATALIE: Noble cousin. *(she withdraws her hand)*

PRINCE: Natalie ... *(pause)* What will you do now? ... From now on?

43

NATALIE: I don't know. The very ground I stand on is destroyed. My father and mother rest in graves in Amsterdam. Dortrecht, our estate, lies in ruins. Prince Moritz, my cousin, under constant attack by the Spanish tyrant, can scarce protect his own family. And now the last support to which I clung like a fragile vine to a strong wall has collapsed.

PRINCE: *(putting an arm around her waist)* My dear friend! If this hour were not dedicated to our mourning I would say: enlace those tender branches here, around this heart that has spent lonely years yearning for their sweet fragrance.

NATALIE: My dear, beloved friend.

PRINCE: Will you? Will you?

NATALIE: ... If I may take root deep in its core.

(she lays her head on his chest)

PRINCE: What? What did you say?

NATALIE: Go now!

PRINCE: Yes! Into its core! Deep into the heart's core!

(he kisses her, but she breaks away)

PRINCE: Dear God! if only he, the man we mourn, were here to witness this alliance. If only we could humbly ask of him, Father, give us your blessing.

(He covers his face with his hands. Natalie goes back to the Electress.)

Scene 6

A sergeant rushes in.

SERGEANT: My Prince, how dare I by the living God report the rumor that the Elector lives!

PRINCE: He lives!

SERGEANT: Count Sparren just arrived here with the news.

NATALIE: My God! Mother, did you hear that?

(she throws herself at the Electress's feet and embraces her)

PRINCE: No! Speak up, man. Who told you this?

SERGEANT: George Von Sparren, who saw him with his own eyes, safe and sound at Hackelburg with Truchss's regiment.

PRINCE: Quick! Run, old man, and bring him here to me! *(the sergeant leaves)*

Scene 7

ELECTRESS: Oh, do not plunge me twice into the abyss.

NATALIE: No, dear mother.

ELECTRESS: Friedrich is alive?

45

NATALIE: *(supporting her with both hands)* You have returned to life's happy heights.

(Count Von Sparren and the sergeant enter)

SERGEANT: *(stepping forward)* Here is the officer, sir.

PRINCE: Count Von Sparren, you have seen his majesty alive and well with Truchss's regiment at Hackelburg?

VON SPARREN: Yes, noble Prince, in the parsonage, surrounded by his staff, where he was giving orders for the burial of the dead from both sides.

LADIES-IN-WAITING: *(embracing each other)* Thank God!

ELECTRESS: Oh, daughter!

NATALIE: It's almost too much joy.

(she buries her head in her aunt's lap)

PRINCE: But I saw it myself! With all my men! Saw the cannon fire. Saw him fall with his horse.

VON SPARREN: It's true the horse and rider fell. But it was not his majesty, my Prince, who rode that horse.

PRINCE: Not him?

NATALIE: A miracle.

PRINCE: Explain! Everything! Your words weigh heavy, like gold, on my chest.

VON SPARREN: Listen to the saddest tale you'll ever hear. His majesty, deaf to every warning, again insisted on riding the dazzling white horse that his groom, Froben, brought back from England. And, as usual, every enemy weapon trained on him. Bullets, grenades, shrapnel—a river of death. Even his own staff couldn't get within a hundred feet of him. But he bravely, calmly, swam through the destructive tide headed for its very source.

PRINCE: Yes, it was a frightful sight.

VON SPARREN: Froben, who was the first to follow him, calls out to me, "I curse myself for buying that white horse. Costly as he was, I'd give another fifty ducats now if I could turn the white to gray." Mad with worry he shouts, "Majesty, your horse is shying; I beg permission to take him back for further training," then jumps from his own horse and grabs the stallion's reins. His majesty dismounts and with a smile, says, "The art you wish to teach this horse will take him longer than the day to learn. Hide him from the enemy in those hills where they can't see his faults." Then he mounts Froben's horse, turns, and resumes his mission. But no sooner does Froben make the change than deadly fire from the field cuts him down, a martyr to fidelity. For him, then, all was still.

(short pause)

PRINCE: He has been well paid. If I had ten lives I could not have asked for more.

NATALIE: Brave Froben.

ELECTRESS: An excellent soldier.

NATALIE: A far lesser man would still deserve our tears. *(they weep)*

PRINCE: Enough. To business. Where is the Elector? Is headquarters at Hackelburg now?

VON SPARREN: I beg your pardon, Prince. His majesty has gone to Berlin. All officers are to join him there at once.

PRINCE: Berlin? Is the campaign over, then?

VON SPARREN: I can't believe you haven't heard the news. Count Horn, the Swedish general, is at our camp, and a cease fire is in effect. Unless I misunderstood Marshal Dorfling, peace negotiations are now under way.

ELECTRESS: How gloriously the skies have cleared.

(she rises)

PRINCE: Let's follow to Berlin at once. To save me time I'd appreciate your making room in your carriage. A moment for a brief note to Kottwitz and I'll join you. *(he sits down and writes)*

ELECTRESS: Of course, with all my heart.

(He folds the letter and hands it to the sergeant. Then he turns to the Electress, at the same time putting an arm around Natalie's waist.)

PRINCE: I have a wish that I find hard to talk about. I hope I may confess it on the trip.

NATALIE: *(breaking loose)* Bork! My scarf, please. Quick!

ELECTRESS: You have a wish of me?

BORK: You're wearing it around your neck, my lady.

PRINCE: *(to the Electress)* You can't guess what it is?

ELECTRESS: Not at all.

PRINCE: Really? Not the least bit?

ELECTRESS: *(cutting him short)* No matter. Today I can't say no to any living creature, least of all to you, the hero of the battle. Now let's go.

PRINCE: Your words make me a happy man. May I interpret them the way I'd wish to?

48

ELECTRESS: Let's go, I say. We'll discuss it in the carriage.

PRINCE: Come, give me your arms. Oh divine Caesar. My ladder's placed for me to reach your star.

(He leads the ladies away. All follow.)

Scene 8

Berlin. A square in front of the old castle. In the background, the royal chapel, a staircase in the front. Bells ring.
We see, inside the church, Froben's body carried to and placed in a magnificent catafalque. Enter, on the square, the Elector, Dorfling, Hennings, Truchss, and other officers. General public in the church and on the square.

ELECTOR: The officer who ordered the attack, on his own, prior to my command, allowed the Swedes to retreat before Hennings could destroy the bridge. No matter who that was, he's guilty of a capital offense and shall be tried by a military court. You say the Prince of Homburg was not in command?

TRUCHSS: That's my understanding, your highness.

ELECTOR: Who confirms this?

TRUCHSS: His cavalrymen. They swear the Prince took a fall from his horse before the battle started. They saw his extensive head and leg wounds being tended to in a church.

ELECTOR: All right. Our victory today was brilliant, and I'll thank God for it tomorrow at the altar.

49

But even if it was ten times greater, it does not justify the crime despite our lucky outcome. There are other battles to fight after this one. The law must be obeyed. I say again: whoever it was that led that charge has forfeited his head. I summon him to military court. Now, my friends, to church.

Scene 9

Enter the Prince of Homburg carrying three Swedish flags, Colonel Kottwitz with two flags, and Hohenzollern, Goltz, and Reuss with one flag each. Other men with flags, drums, and standards.

DORFLING: *(sees the Prince)* The Prince of Homburg! Truchss, do you see this?

ELECTOR: *(startled)* Where have you come from, Prince?

PRINCE: *(stepping forward)* From Fehrbellin, my Lord, and bring you trophies of our victory.

(he lays the flags at the Elector's feet; the others follow suit)

ELECTOR: *(puzzled)* I hear that you were gravely wounded ... Count Truchss?

PRINCE: *(cheerfully)* I beg your pardon?

TRUCHSS: I don't believe this....

PRINCE: My horse did fall—before the battle started. I did have this hand bandaged by an army surgeon. But I'd hardly call this wounded.

ELECTOR: So you led the cavalry?

PRINCE: *(staring)* I did, of course. You haven't heard? The proof is at your feet.

ELECTOR: Take his sword. He's under arrest.

FIELD MARSHAL: *(shocked)* Whose sword?

ELECTOR: *(stepping over flags)* Greetings, Kottwitz.

TRUCHSS: *(aside)* I'm damned!

KOTTWITZ: By God! I'm completely ...

ELECTOR: *(staring at him)* ... Your glorious harvest has increased our fame. This flag here ... unless I'm mistaken it belongs to the Swedish bodyguard?

(he picks up a flag, unfurls it, and studies it)

KOTTWITZ: Your majesty?

FIELD MARSHAL: My Lord?

ELECTOR: Yes, it is indeed. From the time of King Gustav Adolph. What does the inscription say?

KOTTWITZ: I think it ...

FIELD MARSHAL: Per aspera ad astra.

ELECTOR: That wasn't true at Fehrbellin.

(pause)

KOTTWITZ: *(timidly)* Sire, may I speak?

ELECTOR: Yes, what is it? Take everything, flags, drums, and standards, and hang them on the pillars of the church. I'll use them at tomorrow's festivities.

(the Elector turns to the courtiers, takes their dispatches, and starts reading them)

KOTTWITZ: *(aside)* By God, he's going too far.

(Kottwitz hesitates, then picks up his two flags; the others pick up their flags, leaving the Prince's three flags on the floor. Kottwitz picks them up. Now he has five.)

OFFICER: *(stepping up to the Prince)* Prince, your sword, please.

HOHENZOLLERN: *(he holds his flags as he steps up to the Prince)* Stay calm, friend.

PRINCE: Am I dreaming? Awake? Alive? Is this real?

GOLTZ: Prince, I advise you to hand over your sword and say nothing.

PRINCE: I, a prisoner?

HOHENZOLLERN: Yes, you are.

GOLTZ: You heard him.

PRINCE: And why?

HOHENZOLLERN: *(clipped)* Not now. We warned you, but you plunged into battle prematurely. The order was to stay until commanded.

PRINCE: Help. Friends. Help. I'm losing my mind.

GOLTZ: *(interrupting)* Stay calm.

PRINCE: Then did we lose the battle?

HOHENZOLLERN: *(stamping his foot)* That's beside the point!

PRINCE: *(bitterly)* So! That's it! So!

HOHENZOLLERN: *(backing away)* It won't cost you your head.

GOLTZ: *(also backing away)* You'll probably be out by tomorrow.

(the Elector folds up his dispatches and rejoins his officers)

PRINCE: *(unbuckles his sword)* Already my cousin Friedrich sees himself as Brutus seated on the Roman throne, with the Swedish flags placed in the foreground, and before him on a table, in his painting, the Articles of war. By God, he won't find in me the son who pays him honor from the scaffold. Well, let him play the stony Roman. My heart's old German, used to generosity and love. I pity him, I really do.

ELECTOR: Take him back to headquarters at Fehrbellin and convene his court-martial.

(The Elector enters the church followed by the officers with the flags. As they kneel and pray at Froben's bier, the flags are hung on pillars.)

ACT 3

Scene 1

Fehrbellin. A prison.
The Prince. Two calvalry men stand guard in the
background. Enter Hohenzollern.

PRINCE: Ah, it's you, Heinrich. Greeting, old friend.
I'm free, then?

HOHENZOLLERN: *(startled)* Good God!

PRINCE: What is it?

HOHENZOLLERN: Free? Your sword's returned?

PRINCE: To me? No.

HOHENZOLLERN: How then free?

PRINCE: I thought you ... you were bringing it. No
matter.

HOHENZOLLERN: I'm sorry....

PRINCE: I said it doesn't matter. He must be send-
ing someone else to tell me. *(turns and fetches some
chairs)* Sit down. So. What news? The Elector is
back from Berlin?

HOHENZOLLERN: *(distracted)* Yes, last night.

PRINCE: Everything went well—with the victory cele-
bration? But of course it did. Was the Elector in
the church?

HOHENZOLLERN: Yes, with the Electress and Princess Natalie. The church was ablaze, befitting the occasion. During the Te Deum we could hear the splendid roar of cannon from the castle square. The Swedish flags were hung as trophies from the pillars, and the victory, at the Elector's express command, was credited to you from the pulpit.

PRINCE: I've heard that. You've brought some other news? Your look is far from cheerful.

HOHENZOLLERN: Have you spoken to anyone else yet?

PRINCE: To Goltz, just now at the castle where, as you know, I was standing trial.

(*pause*)

HOHENZOLLERN: Arthur, just how would you describe your present position after all that's happened?

PRINCE: As you do, as Goltz, as the court itself does. The Elector acted according to his duty. Now he'll listen to his heart. "You erred," he'll tell me sternly and mention death and prison. "But now I give you back your freedom...." And then around my victorious sword he'll wind a token of his gratitude—well, all right. Perhaps I don't deserve the token.

HOHENZOLLERN: Oh, Arthur ... (*he stops short*)

PRINCE: What?

HOHENZOLLERN: Are you so sure of him?

PRINCE: Certain. He loves me, like a son. I know it. He's shown it in a thousand ways since early childhood. What's wrong? Why are you so doubtful? Wasn't he pleased even more than I at my growing fame? Hasn't he made me everything I am? Could he be so unloving as to trample into dust the plant that he himself has raised, and only because it bloomed too soon with too much display? I would not believe that from his worst enemy, and even less should you, who know and love him.

HOHENZOLLERN: Arthur, he brought you before a court-martial and you still believe this?

PRINCE: *Because* I stood before it. No one would go that far unless he meant to grant a pardon. There before the bar of justice I believed in him again. Is death the proper penalty for grinding the Swedes to dust two minutes prior to the order? What other crime am I guilty of? How could he summon me before this bench of merciless judges, hooting the funeral march of the firing squad like so many owls, unless he meant to silence them with my pardon? No, my friend. He gathers dark clouds round my head just to dispel them like the sun. Surely I can permit him this caprice.

HOHENZOLLERN: Still, they say the court has passed sentence.

PRINCE: Yes, I've heard. It's death.

HOHENZOLLERN: *(astonished)* You know already?

PRINCE: Goltz was in the court. He told me what happened.

HOHENZOLLERN: Good God! . . . the sentence doesn't upset you?

PRINCE: Me? Not at all.

HOHENZOLLERN: You're raving mad. Why are you so confident?

PRINCE: I know him. *(stands)* Now that's enough. Why should I torture myself with false doubts? *(reflects and sits down; pause)* The judges had to vote for death. Their law requires it. But before he'd carry out that sentence, or expose this heart of mine that loves him to a bullet fired on the signal of some handkerchief, I swear he'd rather bare his own chest and spill his own blood in the dust.

HOHENZOLLERN: But Arthur, I assure you ...

PRINCE: *(resisting)* Come, old friend ...

HOHENZOLLERN: The Marshal ...

PRINCE: *(still resisting)* That's enough.

HOHENZOLLERN: Let me say one thing ... then, if you think it's not important, I'll shut up.

PRINCE: *(turning towards him)* I've told you I know it all. ... All right, what is it?

HOHENZOLLERN: Just a little while ago the Field Marshal himself—it is not the usual practice—delivered the death sentence to the castle. The Elector, instead of granting you an immediate pardon as the law specifically permits, ordered it be brought to him for signature.

PRINCE: So what?

HOHENZOLLERN: So what!

PRINCE: *(pause)* For signature, you say?

HOHENZOLLERN: My word of honor. That's what it was.

PRINCE: The sentence. No, it must have been the minutes....

HOHENZOLLERN: The death sentence.

PRINCE: Who told you that?

HOHENZOLLERN: The Field Marshal himself.

PRINCE: When?

HOHENZOLLERN: Just before I came here.

PRINCE: On his way out?

HOHENZOLLERN: As he was coming down the castle steps. Seeing how very upset I was, he added that all was not lost, that while there's life there's hope. But the paleness of his lips denied the words that issued from them and betrayed his fear that all was over.

PRINCE: *(rising)* Could he ... no! ... could he shelter such a wicked purpose in his heart? Given a diamond, would he trample the donor in the dust because a powerful lens detected a scarcely visible flaw? This act would bleach the warlord of Algeria white, cleanse black Sardanapalus of all sin and give him silver wings, find place for the entire roll of Roman tyrants on the right hand of the Lord like innocent sucklings lost at their mother's breast.

HOHENZOLLERN: *(standing up)* My friend, it's time to face the truth.

PRINCE: And then the Marshal stood there and said nothing?

HOHENZOLLERN: What was left to say?

PRINCE: And I had hope. I trusted him.

HOHENZOLLERN: Have you done anything, knowing or not, that might have threatened his royal pride?

PRINCE: Never!

HOHENZOLLERN: Think about it.

PRINCE: Never. I swear. His very shadow was sacred to me.

HOHENZOLLERN: Arthur, don't be angry if I question that. Count Horn, the Swedish envoy is here. His mission, I'm told, concerns Natalie, Princess of Orange. But something the Electress let slip has deeply embarrassed his highness. It's said the Princess has made another choice. You're not involved in this, are you?

PRINCE: What are you telling me?

HOHENZOLLERN: Well, are you?

PRINCE: I am, my friend, and now all's clear to me. My compact with the Princess is my ruin. It's true that I'm to blame for her refusal, because she is engaged to me.

HOHENZOLLERN: You rash, ignorant fool! What have you done? How often have I loyally warned you.

PRINCE: Heinrich, Friend. Help. Help me or I'm lost.

HOHENZOLLERN: I will. Of course I will. There must be a way out of this. Perhaps you should discuss it with the Electress.

PRINCE: *(turning and calling)* Guard!

CAVALRYMAN: *(in the background)* Sir?

PRINCE: Call your captain.

(he quickly takes a cloak from the wall and puts on a plumed hat that has been lying on the table)

HOHENZOLLERN: *(helping him with the cloak)* This move, carefully done, can save you. If the Elector and the Swedish king can sign a peace for the price we've been discussing, his heart will soon be reconciled and in a few short hours you'll be free.

Scene 2

Enter a captain.

PRINCE: *(to the captain)* Stranz, I'm in your custody. I ask permission to leave the prison for an hour on urgent business.

STRANZ: Prince, you are not in my custody. My orders say you are free to go where you wish.

PRINCE: Strange! Then I'm not a prisoner?

HOHENZOLLERN: *(breaking in)* Good enough, it's the same thing.

PRINCE: Goodbye.

HOHENZOLLERN: His chains go with him.

PRINCE: I'm off to the castle to see my aunt. Two minutes and I'm back.

Scene 3

The Elector's room. Enter the Electress and Natalie.

ELECTRESS: Come along, my dear. Do come. Now is your chance. Count Horn and his party have left the castle, and I see a light in your uncle's room. Slip on your shawl, steal in quietly, and see what you can do to save your friend. *(they turn to leave)*

Scene 4

Enter a lady-in-waiting.

LADY-IN-WAITING: My lady, the Prince of Homburg waits without. I could hardly believe my eyes.

ELECTRESS: My God!

NATALIE: The Prince himself?

ELECTRESS: He's a prisoner.

LADY-IN-WAITING: He's standing at the door in his cloak and hat. He seems very upset. He begs an urgent audience.

ELECTRESS: *(exasperated)* The thoughtless fool. To break his word!

NATALIE: Who knows what drives him here.

ELECTRESS: *(she ponders)* Admit him. *(she sits in a chair)*

Scene 5

The Prince enters.

PRINCE: Mother. *(he kneels at her feet)*

ELECTRESS: Prince, why are you here?

PRINCE: I seek mercy.

ELECTRESS: *(with suppressed emotion)* You are a prisoner yet you dare come here? Why add new offenses to the old?

PRINCE: Are you aware of what has happened to me?

ELECTRESS: I am—of everything. But what can one helpless woman do?

PRINCE: Oh, Aunt, would you speak that way if chill death held you in his icy grip as he does me? You, the Princess Natalie, these ladies, seem to me endowed with heavenly powers— deliverers. I'm ready to embrace the lowly stableboy who tends your horse, the meanest servant, begging him to save me. I'm left alone in God's wide world, deserted, feeble, powerless.

ELECTRESS: You're quite beside yourself. What has happened?

PRINCE: As I came here tonight the torches lit the open grave prepared to receive my bones tomorrow. Dear Aunt, these eyes that gaze upon you now they plan to shroud in darkness. They mean to pierce this breast with deadly bullets.

63

In the market square, windows with a view of this dread deed have been reserved. And this man at the peak of life today, who still views the future as a magic place, tomorrow lies a stinking corpse between two narrow boards with just a tombstone telling you that once he was.

(Natalie, who has been leaning on the shoulder of a lady-in-waiting in the backgroud, sits down at a table and weeps)

ELECTRESS: If this is God's will, my son, you must arm yourself with courage and restraint.

PRINCE: I beg you, God's earth is so fair. Don't let me plunge into the dark before my time has come. If I've done wrong, why must the punishment be bullets? Let him take away my titles, reduce my rank if the law demands it. Discharge me with dishonor from the army. My God, since I have seen my grave, I care only for my life and not my honor.

ELECTRESS: Stand up, my son. Please stand up and take hold of yourself. You're going to pieces.

PRINCE: Not until you promise, Aunt, to humbly go before that proud presence and win me back my life. Your girlhood friend, my mother, when she lay dying in Homburg, gave you my charge. "You are his mother when I am gone," she said. Deeply moved, you knelt at her bedside, kissed her hand, and answered, "He'll be my son, as if I'd borne him." Now I remind you of those words. Go then as though you really were my mother and say, "I beg for mercy, mercy. Set him free." Yes, and then return to me and say, "You are free."

ELECTRESS: *(weeping)* But, my son, I've already done that. But all my pleading was in vain.

PRINCE: Why now I renounce all claims to happiness. I do not wish the hand of Princess Natalie—be sure to tell him that. The tenderness I felt for her is dead. She's free again, free as the doe on the heath to pledge her hand and lips, as if I never lived, and if it happens to be King Gustav of Sweden whom she chooses, I commend her choice. My only wish is to retire to my estates along the Rhine, there to sow and reap, build and rebuild till I drip with sweat. Though I'll be alone I'll thus pursue my rounds as if I really had a wife and child, till evening comes and life wanes and dies.

ELECTRESS: Very well. Now back to prison. That's the first condition of my favor.

(the Prince rises and speaks to Natalie)

PRINCE: Poor girl. You're crying. The rising sun today reveals the death of all your hopes. I was your first love, and your expression tells me true as gold you'll never love another. I have no comforts left myself to tender you. I recommend you join your cousin Thurn in the nunnery. Or search the mountains for a baby with blond curls like mine. Buy him and teach him to stammer "mother" as you press him to your breast. And when he's grown, teach him how to close a dead man's eyes. That is all the happiness you have in store.

(Natalie stands up bravely and puts her hand in his)

NATALIE: Return to your cell, my hero. And on your way, look again, this time calmly, at this grave they've dug for you. It's not one inch deeper, one shade darker than those that lay before you on the battlefield. I remain true to you till death. Meanwhile, I will try to find the words to turn my uncle's heart and free you from your pain.

PRINCE: *(after a pause, he folds his hands in prayer and gazes at her with adoration)* Had you two wings, dear Princess, I would take you for an angel, truly. Oh God! Did I really hear you say you'd appeal for me? Where have you hidden until now that quiver holding arrows of persuasion with which you dare attack his majesty? A ray of hope shines in me again.

NATALIE: God will send me arrows for the fray. But if the Elector feels he cannot change the verdict, cannot, so be it then. Brave man that you are, you will bravely yield. The hero who has won a thousand victories in life will know how to triumph over death.

ELECTRESS: Go. We waste most precious time.

PRINCE: May all the saints protect you. Fare you well. God speed you. Send me word of whatever you achieve, of your success.

ACT 4

Scene 1

The Elector's rooms.
The Elector, papers in hand, is standing at a candlelit
desk. Natalie enters and kneels at some distance from
him. Pause.

NATALIE: Noble Uncle, Prince Friedrich of Brandenburg.

ELECTOR: *(putting his papers aside)* Natalie!

(he tries to raise her up)

NATALIE: No, let me stay ...

ELECTOR: What do you want, my dear?

NATALIE: ... here in the dust at your feet, my
proper station, to plead mercy for my Cousin
Homburg. Not to save him for myself, though I
do confess my heart is his. Let him marry any
he chooses—it's enough for me to know he exists,
free and independent, as a flower gladdens me
because it is alive. This I pray of you, my most
sovereign lord and friend. I know that you will
listen to my prayer.

ELECTOR: *(raising her up)* My dear girl ... how can
you ask such a thing? You know he's committed
a most serious crime.

NATALIE: Oh, Uncle dear ...

67

ELECTOR: Well, did he commit a serious crime ...?

NATALIE: An innocent error, only. That blond and blue-eyed boy should have been forgiven before he had to beg for mercy. You surely won't desert him, if only for his mother's sake, but press him to your heart and say, "Weep not, for you are as dear to me as loyalty." Wasn't it his passion to glorify your name that lured him to overstep the law? And, having done so with the folly of a youth, did he not go on to crush the flaming dragon with the fire of a man? First place a crown upon that head, then take that head away? History will not fathom such an act from you that one could almost call inhuman. For God has made no gentler man than you.

ELECTOR: Listen, my darling child, if I were a tyrant, your words, I strongly feel, would melt my iron heart. But since I'm not, how, I ask you, can I by fiat overturn the judgment of my court? What precedent would that establish?

NATALIE: For whom, for you?

ELECTOR: For me? No, not for me. Is nothing higher in your philosophy, dear girl, than me? What about that divine ideal we call, in camp, the Fatherland?

NATALIE: My Lord, why this concern? The Fatherland? Surely it will not be destroyed by one merciful act. Perhaps for you, raised a soldier, to overrule the court denotes disorder. To me it is the highest order. I know the laws of war must be respected, but so must tender feelings. The Fatherland you founded, Uncle, stands, a solid fortress. It can weather storms more dangerous than this. The future, the children of your children, will see it grow, expand in beauty,

68

battlements and towers, like a fairy land, a joy to friends, a terror to our foes. It does not need the mortar of a good friend's blood to hold together after my splendid, peaceful uncle's reign.

ELECTOR: Does your Cousin Homburg think as you do?

NATALIE: Cousin Homburg?

ELECTOR: Does he agree it's all the same for the Fatherland if caprice rules over the law?

NATALIE: That child!

ELECTOR: Well, does he?

NATALIE: Dear Uncle, tears are my only answer.

ELECTOR: *(surprised)* My dear girl, what has happened?

NATALIE: *(hesitant)* The only thing he thinks of now is rescue. He sees the rifle barrels of his executioners, and all desires but the one to live are numbed in him. He'd see all Brandenburg sink in a storm of lightning and thunder and not ask what was happening. Oh, Uncle, what a hero's heart you've humbled.

(she turns away, weeping)

ELECTOR: *(totally amazed)* No, my dearest Natalie. He begs for mercy? Impossible.

NATALIE: If only you had not condemned him.

ELECTOR: No, answer me. He begs for mercy? Good God! What's happened, child? Why are you crying? You spoke to him? Tell me everything. You spoke to him?

NATALIE: *(leaning on his chest)* Yes, just now in my aunt's apartments. He crept there, imagine, in the dark, distraught and timid in his cloak and hat, a wretched, ignoble sight. I think no hero in history could sink so low. I am a woman who's frightened even by a little worm that comes too close. But death, even in the shape of a hideous lion, would not find me so resourceless, crushed, and unheroic. What then is greatness? What is glory?

ELECTOR: *(confused)* So. Then take heart, my child. He's free.

NATALIE: What, your highness?

ELECTOR: He's pardoned. I'll issue the papers immediately.

NATALIE: Is is really true?

ELECTOR: You've heard me.

NATALIE: He's pardoned? He won't die?

ELECTOR: I swear it on my word of honor. How can I deny the views of such a warrior? If he tells me the sentence is unjust—you know I have the highest respect for the Prince's feelings—I'll set it aside and he'll be free. *(he brings her a chair)* Wait, just a moment. *(he sits at the table and writes)*

NATALIE: *(aside)* Oh heart, why are you beating so against your cage?

ELECTOR: *(writing)* Is the Prince still at the castle?

NATALIE: No. He has returned to prison.

(the Elector finishes his letter, seals it, and brings it to Natalie)

ELECTOR: My Natalie weeps. And I, responsible for her happiness, bring clouds of sadness to her

70

eyes instead. *(puts his arm around her)* Would you like to bring this to him yourself?

NATALIE: To the prison?

ELECTOR: *(pressing the letter into her hand)* Yes, why not? *(calls)* Guards!

(enter guards)

Summon the coach. The Princess has some business with the Prince of Homburg.

(exit guards)

He can thank you, in person, for his life. *(embraces her)* Now, am I forgiven?

NATALIE: *(pause)* I don't know, nor want to know, my lord, what moved you suddenly to be so merciful. But I feel in my heart you would not toy with me. The letter, however it may say it, contains, I think, a pardon. For this I thank you. *(kisses his hand)*

ELECTOR: It does indeed, my dear, as surely as the Prince wishes a pardon.

Scene 2

The Princess's apartment. Enter Princess Natalie, two ladies-in-waiting, and Captain Reuss.

NATALIE: *(hurriedly)* You have something for me from my regiment, Count Reuss? Can it wait?

REUSS: *(holding out a letter)* A letter from Colonel Kottwitz, madam.

71

NATALIE: Quick then, give it to me. What does he say?

(she opens it)

REUSS: A petition to his majesty, on behalf of our Prince of Homburg, frank but respectful, as you'll see.

NATALIE: *(reading)* "A most humble entreaty of the Princess of Orange regiment" *(pause)* ... and who wrote this?

REUSS: Colonel Kottwitz, as you can see from the clumsy writing. And his noble name heads the list.

NATALIE: And the thirty signatures following his ...?

REUSS: The rest of the officers, madam, in order of rank.

NATALIE: And why have you brought it to me?

REUSS: To respectfully request that as our chief you add your signature, on the first line, left blank for that purpose.

NATALIE: I hear his highness on his own is pardoning the Prince, which makes this unnecessary.

REUSS: *(delighted)* What? Really?

NATALIE: Still, I won't refuse you. Wisely used, this sheet of paper could tip the scales in his majesty's view of this matter. He may even welcome it as a useful pretext. *(about to sign)*

REUSS: We shall be in your debt.

NATALIE: *(looking up)* The only regiment I see is mine. Where are the Bomsdorf cuirassiers, Goltz, and the Anhelt Pless dragoons?

72

REUSS: It's not, as you may fear, because their hearts beat more faintly than ours. Unfortunately, Kottwitz has been stationed far away in Arnstein, separated from these other regiments stationed here. There is no safe and easy way for this petition to travel.

NATALIE: And so it has too little weight. Are you certain, Count, if you asked the officers stationed here, would they join in this petition?

REUSS: To the last man, madam. Not only the whole cavalry but, I believe, the entire army of Brandenburg—and easily.

NATALIE: *(after a pause)* Then why not dispatch some officers to the camps to do that?

REUSS: Forgive me, but the Colonel has refused to do that. He says he will do nothing which could be misconstrued.

NATALIE: A peculiar man: now bold, now fearful. Luckily I just remembered: his majesty designated me to order Kottwitz back from Arnstein where the stabling is too limited. I must write those orders now.

(she sits down and writes)

REUSS: Perfect, madam. Nothing could help our cause more.

NATALIE: *(while writing)* Then take advantage of it, Count.

(she finishes writing, seals the envelope, and rises)

Meanwhile, understand this letter stays in your dispatch case. Don't rush off to Arnstein or deliver this to Kottwitz until you hear from me.

(She hands him the letter. A guard enters.)

73

GUARD: Madam, the carriage ordered by his majesty is ready in the courtyard.

NATALIE: Bring it to the door! I'll be right there.

(Pause. Deep in thought, she takes her gloves from the table and puts them on.)

Count, I must speak to the Prince. There's room in my carriage. Perhaps you'd like to escort me.

REUSS: I would be honored, madam.

(he offers her his arm)

NATALIE: *(to the ladies-in-waiting)* Follow me, dear friends. Perhaps once there I'll decide to send that letter.

(exit)

Scene 3

The Prince hangs up his hat and drops sadly to some cushions on the floor.

PRINCE: Life's a journey, says the holy man, but the trip is short. From six feet above the ground to six feet under it. I'd prefer to pause halfway there. Today your head's held high, tomorrow it sinks trembling to your breast, the next day it lies beside your heel. They say the sun shines there as well as on even fairer fields. I'm sure that's true. The pity is, the eye that should be viewing all these glories rots before it can look.

74

Scene 4

Enter Princess Natalie, Reuss, and ladies-in-waiting, preceded by a guard with a torch.

GUARD: Her highness, Princess Natalie of Orange.

PRINCE: *(rising)* Natalie!

GUARD: And here she comes.

NATALIE: *(motions with her head to Reuss)* If you would leave us for a moment ...

(exit Reuss and guard)

PRINCE: Your ladyship.

NATALIE: My dearest cousin.

PRINCE: Tell me what brings you here. How does it look?

NATALIE: Good, just as I promised. You're pardoned, free. Here is his letter, confirming it.

PRINCE: Impossible! I must be dreaming.

NATALIE: Read it, read the letter and see.

PRINCE: *(reading aloud)* My Prince of Homburg. When I arrested you for your untimely attack, I believed it to be my duty; I was sure you approved. If you believe yourself unjustly treated, tell me so in two words and I'll return your sword at once.

(Natalie turns pale. Pause. The Prince looks at her questioningly.)

75

NATALIE: *(with forced gaiety)* Well, that's it then. Just send the words. Dear, sweet friend.

(she presses his hand)

PRINCE: Your highness.

NATALIE: Oh, what a blissful moment to be with you. Take this pen and write!

PRINCE: This is his signature?

NATALIE: A single F. That's how he signs. Bork, let's all rejoice. I knew it. His generosity is boundless as the sea. Get the Prince a chair. He'll reply at once.

PRINCE: He says if I believe ...

NATALIE: *(interrupting)* Of course. Hurry! Sit down! I'll dictate your reply.

(she pushes a chair up behind him)

PRINCE: I want to read the letter again.

NATALIE: *(tearing it from his hand)* Why? You've seen your grave yawning at you with open jaws. You're wasting precious time. Sit down and write!

PRINCE: *(smiling)* You say that grave's a panther poised to pounce on me.

(he sits down and picks up a pen)

NATALIE: *(turning away and starting to cry)* If you don't want me to be angry, write, now!

(The Prince writes. Pause. He tears up the letter and throws it under the table.)

PRINCE: A stupid start.

(He takes another piece of paper. Natalie retrieves the first one.)

NATALIE: How can you say that? My God, it's very good, excellent.

PRINCE: (muttering to himself) Wording fit for a scoundrel, not a prince. A different turn of phrase ...

(Pause. He reaches for the Elector's letter which Natalie holds in her hand.)

PRINCE: What did he actually say in his letter?

NATALIE: (pulling it away) Nothing ... at all.

PRINCE: Please give it to me.

NATALIE: You've already read it.

PRINCE: (grabbing it) Yes, but I want to see exactly how to answer.

NATALIE: (aside) Great God, now he's done for.

PRINCE: (shocked) Look at this. Astounding. You must have missed this part.

NATALIE: No, I didn't. Which part?

PRINCE: He says it's my decision.

NATALIE: Yes ...

PRINCE: That's chivalrous of him. The action of a noble heart.

NATALIE: He's infinitely generous. Now you must repay him by agreeing to his request. It's only a formality, but he needs your answer. As soon as he has it, the matter's over.

PRINCE: (putting the letter aside) No, my love, I want to sleep on this.

NATALIE: I don't understand this wavering. Why?

77

PRINCE: (*emotional, rising from the chair*) Please, don't ask that. You haven't really understood this letter. I cannot claim he's treated me unfairly. If you force me to reply now, my answer is, "You've treated me with perfect justice."

(*he sits down at the table again with arms folded, studying the letter*)

NATALIE: You're out of your mind. What are you saying?

(*she bends over him, deeply moved*)

PRINCE: (*pressing her hand*) Wait a minute, I think ... (*he reflects*)

NATALIE: What do you think?

PRINCE: I begin to see what I must write.

NATALIE: Homburg!

PRINCE: (*taking pen*) I'm listening. What is it?

NATALIE: My dear friend. I respect this impulse of yours, but I swear the regimental guns stand ready to deliver your funeral rites over the mound of an unfeeling grave. If nobility prevents you from opposing this sentence, I assure you he will, sublimely and full of pity, have you shot.

PRINCE: (*writing*) It doesn't matter.

NATALIE: Doesn't matter!?

PRINCE: He can do as he pleases. I do what I must do.

NATALIE: (*frightened, she steps toward the Prince*) You senseless man. You can't be writing ...

PRINCE: (*finishing*) ... signed, "Homburg: the twelfth day of the month, at Fehrbellin." Done. Franz!

(he folds the letter in an envelope and seals it)

NATALIE: Great God in heaven!

PRINCE: *(rising)* Take this to the castle, to his majesty.

(exit the servant)

He acts so nobly with me I must prove worthy of it. I feel guilt, great guilt. If his mercy demands I argue for a pardon, then I abjure a pardon.

NATALIE: *(kissing him)* Take this kiss! And if right now a dozen bullets shot you down, I'd be compelled to shout, with joy even as I wept, that you have pleased me. Meanwhile, since you must do as your heart bids, it follows so must I. Count Reuss!

(the courier opens the door; Reuss enters)

REUSS: Madam?

NATALIE: To Arnstein, sir. Give Colonel Kottwitz his letter. The Elector commands the regiment to march. I expect them here before midnight. *(exit)*

ACT 5

Scene 1

A room in the castle.
Enter the Elector, half dressed, Count Truchss, Hohen-
zollern, and Goltz. Pages with torches.

ELECTOR: Kottwitz! With the Princess's troops? Here
in town?

TRUCHSS: *(opening the window)* Yes, your majesty.
They're standing outside the castle.

ELECTOR: Well, solve this riddle for me. Who called
them here?

HOHENZOLLERN: I don't know, my lord.

ELECTOR: He should be in Arnstein. That's where I
assigned him. Quickly, one of you, bring him
here.

TRUCHSS: He should be here at any moment, sir.

ELECTOR: Where is he?

GOLTZ: In the town hall, I hear, where every officer
serving under you is meeting.

ELECTOR: Why? What for?

HOHENZOLLERN: That I don't know.

TRUCHSS: Sir, we request permission to join our
fellow officers.

ELECTOR: At the town hall?

HOHENZOLLERN: Yes, sir, we gave our word we would appear.

ELECTOR: *(after a brief pause)* You are dismissed!

GOLTZ: Come, my friends.

(exit)

Scene 2

Elector. Later. Two servants.

ELECTOR: Singular, surely. If I were the Dey of Tunis I'd sound the alarm at such an ambiguous situation. I'd prepare the gallows, bar the gate, and prime the cannon. But it's only old Hans Kottwitz from Prignitz! And though he comes here without leave, still I'll act in proper Brandenburg tradition. I'll take him by one of his remaining silver hairs and quietly lead him and his twelve squadrons back to Arnstein. Why wake this sleeping town?

(He steps over to the window again for a moment, then returns to the table and rings. Two servants enter.)

ELECTOR: Run over and find out what's going on at the town hall. Pretend you're asking for yourself.

SERVANT: Yes, my lord. *(exit)*

ELECTOR: And you, my uniform.

(The servant exits and returns with all the ornate trappings of office. The Elector starts to don them.)

Scene 3

Enter Field Marshal Dorfling.

FIELD MARSHAL: Your majesty, it's a rebellion!

ELECTOR: Dorfling, please. You know how I hate people bursting in here unannounced. Now what is it?

FIELD MARSHAL: Sir, I apologize, but this is urgent. Colonel Kottwitz has marched here without orders. He's meeting with a hundred officers in the Hall of Knights. They're circulating a petition to deny your prerogatives.

ELECTOR: I know all about it. It must be a demand to spare Homburg.

FIELD MARSHAL: Exactly.

ELECTOR: Well, good. I sympathize with their position.

FIELD MARSHAL: I hear these madmen mean to hand you this petition here, today. And if you remain unyielding—dare I tell you—they intend to free him by force.

ELECTOR: *(gravely)* Who told you this?

FIELD MARSHAL: A woman you can rely on completely—Lady Retzow, my wife's cousin. Last night at her uncle's house, the Bailiff Retzow, she heard some officers, just arrived from camp, boasting of this reckless plot.

ELECTOR: I'd have to hear this from a man before I'd believe it. All it needs to shield him from

83

these young heroes is the sight of me at his prison door.

FIELD MARSHAL: Sir, I entreat you, if you have any thought of pardoning the Prince, do it now before some disaster occurs. You know how every army loves its hero. Don't let what now is just a spark become a ravaging fire. Kottwitz and the others don't know I've loyally warned you. Before they come, return the Prince's sword, which as a matter of fact he deserves. Then the papers can report a noble deed and not a cruel one.

ELECTOR: First I must hear from the Prince. Since his arrest was not arbitrary, his release cannot be. When the gentlemen arrive, I'll speak to them.

FIELD MARSHAL: *(aside)* Damn, he's armed against every one of my arrows.

Scene 4

Enter two guards. One is holding a letter.

GUARD: Sir, Colonel Kottwitz, Hennings, Truchss, and others request an audience.

ELECTOR: *(to the other guard)* From the Prince of Homburg?

GUARD: Yes, your majesty.

ELECTOR: Who gave it to you?

GUARD: The Swiss sentry at the gate, given it by the Prince's orderly.

(The Elector steps to the table and reads the letter. He calls a page.)

ELECTOR: Yes, Prittwitz, bring me the Prince's death warrant.... Oh, also the safe-conduct pass for the Swedish envoy, Count Horn.

(exit the page; to the first guard)

Show Count Kottwitz and his group in.

Scene 5

Enter Kottwitz, Hennings, Truchss, Hohenzollern, Von Sparren, Reuss, Goltz, Stranz, and other officers. Kottwitz holds the petition.

KOTTWITZ: Permit me, your majesty, humbly to submit this document on behalf of the entire army.

ELECTOR: Before we get to that, Kottwitz, tell me, who ordered you back to Fehrbellin?

KOTTWITZ: *(staring at him)* With the dragoons?

ELECTOR: With the regiment. I assigned you to Arnstein.

KOTTWITZ: Sir, your orders brought me here.

ELECTOR: What? Show them to me.

KOTTWITZ: Here, my lord.

ELECTOR: *(reading)* Signed, "Natalie—Fehrbellin—by order of my uncle, His Majesty, Friedrich."

KOTTWITZ: Good Lord, my Prince, I can't believe you don't know about this.

ELECTOR: No, no, I mean who brought the order to you?

KOTTWITZ: Count Reuss.

ELECTOR: *(after a short pause)* In any case, I welcome you! You and your twelve squadrons have been chosen to pay final honors to the condemned Prince of Homburg in the morning.

KOTTWITZ: *(stunned)* What, your majesty!

ELECTOR: *(handing back the order)* Your regiment remains in front of the castle, *(quotes)* "In darkness and in mist."

KOTTWITZ: ... "darkness and mist"? Forgive me, sire ...

ELECTOR: Why haven't you found quarters for your men?

KOTTWITZ: My Lord, they have been quartered, right here in Fehrbellin as you ordered.

ELECTOR: Well, you've certainly been quick to find stables. Good. Again I welcome you. Now what brings you here? You have some news for me?

KOTTWITZ: Sire, a petition from your loyal army.

ELECTOR: Present it.

KOTTWITZ: But the words you said a moment ago have crushed my hopes.

ELECTOR: Then words can mend them. *(reads)* "Petition begging supreme mercy for our general, indicated by capital letters, Prince Friedrich of Hessen-Homburg, sentenced now to death." *(looks up)* A noble name, gentlemen, a name worthy of such great support. *(looks down at the paper)* Tell me, who wrote this?

KOTTWITZ: I did, sire.

ELECTOR: Does the Prince know about it?

KOTTWITZ: Not at all. It was initiated and written among ourselves.

ELECTOR: A moment's patience, please.

(he steps over to the table and reads; pause)

Hmm! Curious! A veteran like you defends the Prince's action, justifies the attack on Wrangel without my order.

KOTTWITZ: Your majesty, that's where Kottwitz stands.

ELECTOR: You thought otherwise on the battlefield.

KOTTWITZ: My judgment was wrong. I should have trusted the Prince's skills in the art of war. The Swedish left was breaking with reinforcements coming from the right. If he had waited for your orders they would have gained new footholds in the ravines, and you would have no victory to celebrate.

ELECTOR: So, that's how you interpret it. The fact is, I sent Colonel Hennings to take the bridgehead guarding Wrangel's rear. If you had not countered my orders, Hennings would have attacked, burned the bridges, and his men would have been entrenched along the Rhyn. Wrangel's army would have been annihilated in the swamps.

KOTTWITZ: Sir, only novices, not leaders like yourself, expect to win a total war. Until today you were content with fortune's grant. What more could you ask from one day's work? The dragon threatening our land is driven away with bloodied head. What does it matter if he lies licking his wounds for two weeks in the sand? And now we've learned the secret of beating him, we long to take him on again. Just one more fight with Wrangel, man to man, and he's finished, back to his Baltic lair forever. Rome, sir, was not built in a day.

ELECTOR: Foolish man. How can you assure that total victory if anyone can take the reins of my battle chariot on a whim? Do you claim luck will always be there to reward insubordination? This victory's illegitimate, Fortune's bastard child. I want the mother of my own crown, the law, to bear me a long line of victories.

KOTTWITZ: Majesty, the highest law to move your general's hearts is not the expression of your will. It is the Fatherland, it is the crown, it is you yourself on whose head that crown rests. What matters the rule by which the enemy is beaten so long as his banners fall at your feet? The rule that beats him is the highest rule. Should this army, so passionately loyal to you, become an unthinking instrument, like the lifeless sword at your golden belt? What a poor soul it was that first taught that. Statesmen, guided by one example where pure emotion proved destructive, forget ten others in our history where it won the day. Do I shed my blood on the battlefield for pay in cash or honor? God forbid. I value it more highly. I do it for myself alone, freely, independently, taking delight in your magnificence and in the glory of your name. That's the price for which I pay my heart. Assume you execute the Prince for this illegal victory and one day, shepherding my squadron through a valley, I see a chance for victory not called for in the plan, by God I'd be a scoundrel if I didn't

88

do as he did, eagerly. And if you, rule book in your hand, said, "Kottwitz, you have forfeited your head," I'd say, I knew that, sir, take it. When I swore loyalty to your crown, my head was included in my oath. I give you nothing that's not yours already.

ELECTOR: You, wonderful old man, are too much for me. You tempt me with your cunning oratory. Especially since I so sympathize with what you say. So to plead my case I'll call another advocate in my defense whose pleadings should end our debate.

(he rings and a servant enters)

The Prince of Homburg! Have him brought at once.

(exit the servant)

I'm sure he'll teach you now what discipline and duty mean. At least his letter denies the schoolboy views on freedom that you have so glibly voiced.

(he returns to the table and picks up a paper)

KOTTWITZ: What did he say? Whom did he send for?

HENNINGS: The Prince himself?

TRUCHSS: Impossible!

(the officers come together nervously to confer)

ELECTOR: Whose is this second letter?

HOHENZOLLERN: Mine, sir.

ELECTOR: *(reading)* ... proof that the Elector himself must take blame for the Prince's—by God, that's insolent. You say I'm responsible for the Prince's crime?

89

HOHENZOLLERN: Yes, your majesty. I, Hohenzollern.

ELECTOR: Well, this is better than a fairy tale. One man says the Prince is innocent. The next says that I'm the guilty one. How do you propose to prove it?

HOHENZOLLERN: Your majesty remembers the night we found the Prince asleep under the plane trees in the garden? Surely he was dreaming, laurel wreath in hand, of next day's victories. You, to test his heart, took the wreath and, smiling, wound your gold chain round its leaves and handed it to your noble niece. Blushing, our Prince rose to claim that trophy from the dear hands of this wondrous vision. But you, retreating quickly with the Princess, vanished through the open door—chain wreath and maid and all, vanished. He stood alone, encapsuled by the night, holding in his hand a glove whose owner was unknown.

ELECTOR: Glove? What glove?

HOHENZOLLERN: Sir, allow me to finish. This was a joke to us, but I soon learned it meant much more to him. I circled back and casually joined him. And though I woke him to the real world, the memory suffused him with an unutterable joy. You can't imagine anything more touching. He described it all to me in perfect detail. So vivid a dream, he was convinced, had to be a sign from heaven that everything he'd seen— lady, wreath, and chain—would be granted him next day by the God of Battle.

ELECTOR: How strange. What about the glove?

HOHENZOLLERN: Yes, now he's puzzled in his mind. What he'd thought a dream is somehow made real by the object in his hand. He knows not what to think. A lady's glove, but he had seen no lady, nor spoke to any in the garden. Just then I come and interrupt his musings and call him for the briefing. Suspending what he cannot understand, unheeding, he puts the glove away.

ELECTOR: And then?

HOHENZOLLERN: Then with pen and notebook he goes in to give his full attention to the Marshal's orders. By chance, the Princess and your noble wife are in the room, preparing to leave. Can you imagine his amazement when the Princess started searching for the very glove he has inside his coat? Repeatedly the Field Marshal calls his name. "What are my orders?" he replies, trying to collect his thoughts. But faced with all these miracles, a bolt of heaven wouldn't ... *(he stops short)*

ELECTOR: Was it the Princess's glove?

HOHENZOLLERN: Of course.

(the Elector ponders, deeply)

He stands there like a stone, pencil in hand, seemingly alive, but every feeling, as if struck by magic, gone. Not until next morning, with cannonfire thundering overhead, does he revive and ask me, "Heinrich, at the briefing yesterday, what were my orders from Dorfling?"

FIELD MARSHAL: My lord, I'll strongly confirm this story. The Prince did not take in a word of what I said. I've never seen him so distracted.

ELECTOR: And so, if I correctly understand your higher logic, had I not so questionably sported with this helpless dreamer's mind, he would

91

have been attentive at the briefing and obedient on the battlefield. That is your meaning? Come now, isn't it?

HOHENZOLLERN: My lord, I leave that conclusion to you.

ELECTOR: You are a fool, a muddled fool! Suppose you hadn't called me to the garden? I would not have been curious, not have played that harmless joke on the dreamer. So by your logic, I say you are guilty of this crime. Oh, the Delphic wisdom of my officers!

HOHENZOLLERN: I've said enough, sir. I'm certain you've been affected by my words.

Scene 6

Enter an officer.

OFFICER: The Prince, my lord, will be here shortly.

ELECTOR: Good, show him in.

OFFICER: A few more minutes, sir. He stopped at the cemetery gate and asked to enter.

ELECTOR: In the churchyard?

OFFICER: Yes, my lord.

ELECTOR: Why?

OFFICER: I don't really know. Apparently he wished to see the grave which you have ordered for him.

(the officers gather and confer)

ELECTOR: Oh, well, when he arrives, admit him at once.

(he goes to the table and leafs through the papers)

TRUCHSS: Here he is now, with his guard.

Scene 7

The Prince enters with a guard.

ELECTOR: My dear young Prince, I ask you for your help. This petition has been presented on your behalf by Colonel Kottwitz. Notice it's been signed by a hundred noblemen. It repudiates the verdict of the court and insists that you be freed. Please, I pray you, read it for yourself.

(the Prince studies the document briefly, then turns and looks at the officers)

PRINCE: Kottwitz, dear old friend, your hand. You've done more for me today than I earned from you on the field of battle. But now return to Arnstein to stay. I've thought it over deeply, and I wish to die the death that is decreed.

(he hands back the petition)

KOTTWITZ: *(stunned)* No, my Prince. What are you saying?

HOHENZOLLERN: He wants to die?

TRUCHSS: He cannot, shall not die.

SEVERAL OFFICERS: *(rushing forward)* Majesty, sir, hear us!

PRINCE: Silence! Having breached the sacred code of battle, it is my unalterable wish to glorify that code with my voluntary death in full view of the army. My brothers, how would one more small victory over Wrangel compare to my glorious triumph tomorrow, over the enemy within, over arrogant pride? Let every foreign prince who would enslave us fall and every Brandenburger live a free man on his native soil. This land is his, and all its meadow's splendors, his alone.

KOTTWITZ: *(very moved)* My son. My dearest friend. What can I call you now?

TRUCHSS: Almighty God.

KOTTWITZ: Let me kiss your hand.

(all press around the Prince)

PRINCE: *(to the Elector)* Sovereign, to whom once I had the right to use a familiar name, a privilege I've forfeited, humbly I submit myself to you. Forgive me if I served you too rashly on that fateful day. Now death cleanses me of guilt. At peace and cheerful, I accept my sentence. It would comfort me to know you bear me ill will no longer. And as a sign of this, your grace, grant me one favor in this our final hour.

ELECTOR: Speak, young hero. What is your wish? No matter what it is, I pledge to grant it, on my noble honor.

PRINCE: Do not buy peace from Karl Gustav with your niece's hand. Expel the Swedish envoy with his infamous proposals and let your answer be the sound of guns.

ELECTOR: *(kissing his forehead)* So shall it be. Let this kiss be pledge for that. Why should there be another sacrifice to the war's calamities? From every word you've uttered a victory blooms to crush the enemy. So I'll write to King Gustav: she is the Prince of Homburg's bride, who gave his life for Fehrbellin in honor of its laws. The king must win her on the battlefield against the Prince's ghost still marching with our battle flags in death.

(he kisses him once more and raises him to his feet)

PRINCE: Know, thanks to you, I live again. Now I shall pray that every blessing from the misty thrones of angels on you be showered, joyously. Go and do battle, sir, and conquer the whole world if it defies you—for you are worthy.

ELECTOR: Guard, escort him back to prison!

Scene 8

Natalie, the Electress, ladies-in-waiting, appear at the door.

NATALIE: Please, mother. Please don't speak about decorum. The proper action now is to love him ... my poor, unlucky friend.

PRINCE: *(leaving)* Let's go.

TRUCHSS: *(holding him)* No, my Prince. Never.

(several officers bar the way)

PRINCE: Take me away!

HOHENZOLLERN: My Elector, does your heart really allow ...?

PRINCE: *(breaking free)* Tyrants! Do you want to see me dragged before the firing squad in chains? Let me go! I've settled my accounts with the world. *(he leaves with the guards)*

NATALIE: *(leaning on her aunt)* Oh, earth, take me to your bosom. There's no reason more to welcome the sunlight.

Scene 9

FIELD MARSHAL: Good God! Can all this be happening?

(the Elector speaks urgently to an officer, in private)

KOTTWITZ: *(coldly)* My sovereign, after all this, are we dismissed?

ELECTOR: No, not yet. I'll let you know when you're dismissed. *(he glares at him, then takes the papers that the page has brought him from the table and turns to the Field Marshal)* Give this safe conduct to the Swedish count. In three days the war begins again. It is my cousin Homburg's last request which I am bound to honor.

(pause; he glances at the death warrant)

Now judge for yourself, gentlemen. In the past year alone the Prince's careless recklessness has cost me two great victories and flawed a third. Now that he's undergone the schooling of these last few days, would you risk a fourth?

KOTTWITZ AND TRUCHSS: What! Oh, divine ruler...

ELECTOR: Well, will you?

KOTTWITZ: I'm sure, now, you could be tottering at the edge of an abyss and the Prince wouldn't even draw his sword to save your life unless you gave him a specific order.

ELECTOR: *(tearing up the death warrant)* So. Now friends, to the garden.

Scene 10

The castle wall and ramp as in Act 1. Night.
The Prince's guard and its officers are present. The Prince of Homburg, blindfolded, is escorted in by Captain Stranz through the lower gate. We hear the distant beat of funereal drums.

PRINCE: Now, immortality, you are entirely mine. Your radiance, stronger than a thousand suns, pierces my blindfold. Wings grow on my shoulders, my soul soars into the calm silence of the outer spheres. And as a wind-driven ship sees its bright harbor fade away, so all life recedes from me, and only shapes and colors can I make out in the mist.

(The Prince is seated on a bench beneath an oak tree. Captain Stranz moves off and looks up at the ramp.)

How sweet the scent of the violets. Do you smell them, Stranz?

STRANZ: *(returning)* Sir, I believe those are carnations.

PRINCE: Really? How did carnations get here?

STRANZ: I'm not sure. I believe a young girl planted them. Would you like one?

PRINCE: How kind. I'll take it home and put it in water.

Scene 11

Enter the Elector, carrying the laurel wreath wound round with his gold chain. The Electress, Natalie, Dorfling, Kottwitz, Hohenzollern, Goltz, etc. Ladies-in-waiting, officers, and pages with torches on the ramp. Hohenzollern signals Stranz from the balcony with a scarf, and Stranz then moves away from the Prince and speaks to the guards in the background.

PRINCE: Stranz, what is this radiance around me?

STRANZ: *(returning)* Please rise, my Prince.

PRINCE: What is it?

STRANZ: Nothing to fear. I'm only going to remove the blindfold.

PRINCE: Then my suffering will end?

STRANZ: It will. Hail to you and all God's blessings. You are worthy of them.

(The Elector gives the wreath to Natalie, then leads her down the ramp. Ladies and gentlemen follow. Surrounded by torches, Natalie places the wreath on the Prince's head, hangs the chain around his neck, and presses his hand to her heart. The Prince faints.)

NATALIE: Good heavens, he'll die with joy.

HOHENZOLLERN: *(catching him)* Some help, please.

ELECTOR: Let the cannon wake him.

(Cannon shots. A military march. The castle wall suddenly lights up.)

KOTTWITZ: Hurrah. Hurrah for the Prince of Homburg.

OFFICERS: Hip, hip, hoorah. Hip, hip, hoorah. Hip, hip, hoorah. To the hero of Fehrbellin!

(a moment of silence)

PRINCE: No. Tell me, truly. Is this a dream?

KOTTWITZ: Yes, truly. What else could it be?

OFFICERS: To the battle! To arms, to arms!

TRUCHSS: To the battlefield.

FIELD MARSHAL: And victory!

ALL: Destroy the enemies of Brandenburg.

ELEPHANT PAPERBACKS

Literature and Letters
Stephen Vincent Benét, *John Brown's Body*, EL10
James Gould Cozzens, *Castaway*, EL6
James Gould Cozzens, *Men and Brethren*, EL3
Clarence Darrow, *Verdicts Out of Court*, EL2
Floyd Dell, *Intellectual Vagabondage*, EL13
Theodore Dreiser, *Best Short Stories*, EL1
Joseph Epstein, *Ambition*, EL7
André Gide, *Madeleine*, EL8
Sinclair Lewis, *Selected Short Stories*, EL9
William L. O'Neill, ed., *Echoes of Revolt: The Masses,
    1911–1917*, EL5
Ramón J. Sender, *Seven Red Sundays*, EL11
Wilfrid Sheed, *Office Politics*, EL4
Tess Slesinger, *On Being Told That Her Second Husband Has
    Taken His First Lover, and Other Stories*, EL12

Theatre and Drama
Plays for Performance:
    Georges Feydeau, *Paradise Hotel*, EL403
    Henrik Ibsen, *Ghosts*, EL401
    Heinrich von Kleist, *The Prince of Homburg*, EL402